Z IS FOR ZOMBIE

AND DON'T MISS

V IS FOR VAMPIRE,

COMING JUNE 2011!

Z IS FOR ZOMBIE

An Illustrated Guide to the End of the World

ADAM-TROY CASTRO

ILLUSTRATED BY **JOHNNY ATOMIC**

OF LEAGUE ENTERTAINMENT

HARPER Voyager

An Imprint of HarperCollinsPublishers

Z IS FOR ZOMBIE. Text copyright © 2011 by Adam-Troy Castro. Illustrations copyright © 2011 by Johnny Atomic. All rights reserved. Printed in the United States of America. No part of this book may be used or reproduced in any manner whatsoever without written permission except in the case of brief quotations embodied in critical articles and reviews. For information address HarperCollins Publishers, 10 East 53rd Street, New York, NY 10022.

HarperCollins books may be purchased for educational, business, or sales promotional use. For information please write: Special Markets Department, HarperCollins Publishers, 10 East 53rd Street, New York, NY 10022.

FIRST EDITION

DESIGNED BY PAULA RUSSELL SZAFRANSKI

Harper Voyager and design is a trademark of HCP LLC.

Library of Congress Cataloging-in-Publication Data has been applied for.

ISBN 978-0-06-199185-1

11 12 13 14 15 OV/RRD 10 9 8 7 6 5 4 3 2 1

For Bela

—Adam-Troy Castro

For Uncle Tony

—Johnny Atomic

 Is for Apocalypse

It begins on a day like any other. People rise from their beds, kiss their children, and get dressed for their jobs.

Some notice an unsettling change in the air. They won't be able to smell it—at least not yet, though that will come. But they feel the difference with every breath. Though it still fills their lungs and still provides them with whatever life they need to survive, the atmosphere itself has turned cold, less than nourishing to the living things who need to gulp it by the liter in order to keep their blood flowing red. Some say the air feels liquid. Cold. A few, coming close, use the word *stagnant*.

Only a few, the sensitive, come up with the proper word: *damned*.

The truth is that something primal has changed during the night. There have been dark negotiations between those we exalt as gods and those we fear as demons. Treaties have been rewritten. Borders have been redrawn. The territories that once belonged to the realm of life now belong on the wrong side of death.

For those of us living on Earth it's a lot like learning that the government has decided to plow under our homes and neighborhoods using the right of eminent domain, except there's no warning and no appeal and no compensation and no other place to go.

Yes. This is unfair.

It certainly sucks to be us.

B Is for Buried

Some of us are close enough to hear the first stirrings in the earth.

It sounds like shifting soil, because it is.

It's loose dirt rushing in to fill the empty spaces left when bones long yellowed by age stir with the first spark of a force that is not life or death but some terrible compromise between them.

It's the sudden exodus of ants and worms upset by the discovery that the corpses they've broken down for millennia have just developed enough volition to object to that process.

It's the shuddering earth in ten thousand graveyards, where the dirt trembles and swells and then caves in as the things that used to be us begin to claw their way out.

Remember that unctuous salesman at the mortuary, who called cremation a cheaper and healthier alternative?

Remember how you balked at the idea of doing that to dear old Uncle Stu?

You should have listened.

Because here comes Uncle Stu now.

And you thought he smelled bad when he was . . .

ALIVE.

C Is for Cannibalistic

They're hungry.

There's no reason for them to be. After all, they haven't been doing much of anything. And eating shouldn't help them much; their stomachs, intestines, kidneys, and livers are all as dead as the rest of them. The processes that turn protein into energy cannot and will not work inside them. So you'd expect food to be the last thing on their minds, if they had minds.

But this is a day when all the rules of science and logic are suspended.

So they're hungry.

They're nothing *but* hungry.

They yearn for the one thing they'll never have again, which is life, and not just any life, but the very same life they used to have. So they crawl from their graves and funeral homes and mortuary slabs, and they sniff the air, and they sense us, still wide-eyed and complacent as we stumble through the world we thought we knew, and it occurs to them that they've just found a ticket to the afterlife's most sumptuous ambulatory buffet.

Sure, we'll run away.

But that just makes us fast food.

Do you want flies with that?

D Is for Decaying

Remember that basic rule of etiquette, that everybody should always wash up before they come to dinner?

The walking dead have forgotten it.

They're filthy. Not only are they covered with dirt, reeking of formaldehyde, and sporting a nice menagerie of worms and maggots and flies, but they haven't even taken care of their clothing.

Just look at that one, over there. He's covered with rags. And I'm not even sure what kind. Is that design on his chest the remnants of a T-shirt or a tattoo?

They don't even have the common courtesy to wear the wet parts on the inside.

When they enter your neighborhood, it's like having the most obnoxious, messiest, most malodorous family in the entire universe sit down next to you at McDonald's. That is, it would if you constituted the Happy Meal, which you wouldn't, since you might be a meal but won't be very happy.

Be grateful that you can smell them coming.

It might help you live a little bit longer.

E Is for Everywhere

The schools. The hospitals. The military bases. The shopping malls. The highways. The churches. The bed-and-breakfasts. The dark place under the stairs. The closet. The only bridge out of town. The only unflooded tunnel out of Manhattan. Standing right here, next to you. The backseat of the car you just hot-wired in a last-ditch effort to get away. The grocery store you loot for necessary supplies. George Romero's house. (What, you thought they'd treat him with professional courtesy?) High-rise apartment buildings. Armored underground bunkers. Buckingham Palace. Your local comic book store. IKEA. North of you. South of you. West of you. East of you. That stand of trees over there. Just behind that pastoral hill. Both houses of Congress. The refugee ship taking the last survivors of your town to that stocked fortress in the Arctic. And, if you stop reading this book and turn around right now, looking over your shoulder. Not to put too fine a point on it, people, but everywhere we were, they are. Forget any hopes you might have of finding a safe place. There isn't one.

F Is for Fighting Back

In the days that follow, we all find out what we're made of.

This includes those of us who are cornered and eaten right away. The dead don't just teach us that; they provide us with visual aids. See this bleeding thing that one just ripped from your abdominal cavity? That's your liver. Yes, that came from you.

For the rest of us the lesson is more abstract, more a question of inner courage and will to live and speed of learning curve.

If you don't get with the program and start decapitating dead people right away, you might as well give up on any plans for later in the week. Want to whine about it? Want to curl up in a dark place and sob as the shuffling forms gather around you, like a mob of buffet diners all converging on the last hot tray with chicken wings? Sorry. That's not an option. Either you hit the ground running or you hit the ground in pieces.

And unless you're one of those folks with a rack of automatic weapons in your basement, you're also going to have to brush up on your skills at improv . . . which happens to work pretty much the same way when it comes to fighting the undead as it does for comedy troupes. When the time comes you'll find yourself in the spotlight, vastly outnumbered, the center of everybody's attention, with only a heartbeat to come up with a killer idea for whatever lame prop you're trapped with.

Quick! Name a common household item!

G Is for Gruesome

And once you're done impaling your sweet aunt Edna with the sharpened end of a toilet bowl brush, you're going to have to face the nastiest part of the whole thing.

Fighting zombies is messy work.

The one you just fried with that jet of flame from the can of insecticide? He's the reason your ceiling looks like the inside of a microwave oven that hasn't been cleaned for a while. The one you just split down the middle with the chain saw to the face? That's his eye, still blinking at you from the credenza. The one you got with the double-barreled shotgun? That's his frontal lobe, slowly peeling away from the living room chandelier prior to plummeting to the carpet like a saturated sponge.

Sights like these will become tremendously common in the days to come. You'll no doubt see half a dozen things this gross, or more, before breakfast . . . which will incidentally be the main reason why you'll soon fall into the habit of skipping breakfast. Your sausage links with spicy salsa, your corned beef hash, your glass of tomato juice, and your bowl of steaming hot oatmeal will all now come with unfortunate stomach-churning associations. The bad news is that things won't get any more appetizing by lunch. Want to keep up your strength? You're really going to have to get over being such a priss.

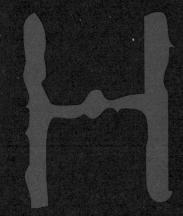

Is for Harold

You're also going to have to keep a sharp eye on Harold. His name might not actually be Harold, but every group of besieged survivors will have one.

Harold's the guy who might have been a valuable member of your neighborhood bowling team, but who turns out after the rising of the dead to be no damned good in a crisis.

A group of you will all be trapped in some isolated farmhouse with the phone lines down and the radio blaring warnings that even the emergency broadcast stations are about to go off the air. You'll be barricading the windows with doors and chopped-up furniture to keep out the hundreds of hungry zombies trying to get in. But you'll run out of doors taken off their hinges before you're even close to fortifying all the possible points of entry, and even as you struggle to block the picture window in the sunroom with the last sheets of scavenged plywood, you'll scream, "It's not going to hold! It's not going to hold! I need more!"

And Harold will shout behind you that he has a door. Here he is helping to hold it in place while you and the rest of your terrified friends finish nailing it up.

It is only when the immediate crisis seems over that you realize that this new door comes complete with street number and mail slot.

It's the *front* door.

Appalled, you all slowly turn around just in time to see the rotting hordes about to engulf you.

That Harold.

He sure could bowl, but he's no damned good in a crisis.

I Is for Innards

We all have a lot of gooey stuff inside us, and one of the nastier things zombies like to do is pull it out while you watch. You don't stand a snowball's chance in hell of maintaining your dignity at a time like this, so you might as well not try. Scream as much as you want, as long as you have lungs to scream with. If you're very, very lucky, your cries might reach the ears of a friend on a rooftop, one with a sniper rifle and enough compassion to put you out of your misery. If not, your troubles are just beginning. Because when you do succumb to your wounds, seconds or minutes or even hours from now, you will soon rise as one of *them* . . . and as much as being undead qualifies as a fate worse than death, being undead with your saucy bits hanging out is even worse. You know how much it sucks to find yourself at your front door clutching an overstuffed grocery bag loaded to the top, as the plastic begins to rip and the contents start to spill out while you're still groping blindly for your keys and it suddenly starts to rain? Now imagine that you can't ever put that frayed plastic bag down because it's your midsection and that the wet things slipping out through that big expanding tear at the bottom are all irreplaceable parts of you. Imagine also that the most mouthwatering meal you've ever hoped to eat is just across the street but leaving the neighborhood in a hurry, and that you have to stumble after it hoping to catch up without dropping anything on the way. We can only stress: it's not so funny when it happens to you.

J Is for Just a Few Random Survivors

As long as you are still alive and fighting for your life, it would be genuinely convenient if the folks you found yourself trapped with were an elite and heavily armed paramilitary force, well versed in the ways of killing. It would be nice if they came from a secret government strike team that has been training in the desert to lead us all back to civilization after the day the zombies rise. It would be nice if one of them was a trained combat surgeon accustomed to performing emergency appendectomies without even pausing to look up when his anesthesiologist threw grenades at the undead things swarming in through the windows. It would be terrific indeed if one of them was a genetically altered supersoldier developed for just this very eventuality, who could wade into an unruly mob of rotting carnivores and decapitate them, one at a time, with nothing but well-aimed kicks to the vertebrae at the base of the neck. It would be amazing if one of them was a brilliant scientist who's developed a handheld electronic device that emits a subsonic signal that repels the dead as much as their smell repels you. Somebody, somewhere, will be lucky enough to be trapped in a room filled with those types. But random chance dictates that you will spend your own last days fighting alongside a mobile phone salesman, a zither player, a sommelier, and a guy who knows the world is ending but still can't talk about anything but his favorite episode of *Star Trek*. Try not to be bitter. They're probably just as upset to be stuck with you.

K Is for Killing

As long as the dead continue to rise and as long as they continue to shuffle toward you intent on making you one of them, you will inevitably embrace other disposal methods just to keep from going insane. If you live long enough you'll bludgeon them with baseball bats, fry them with waffle irons, flatten them with steamrollers, blow them to pieces with fragmentation grenades, and impale them on fiberglass swordfish. There will come a time when you find yourself appreciating the cruel genius of the survivor in that bombed-out ruin across the way, the one who set all those noose snares attached to trebuchets that fling the occasional interloping corpse into the next county. If you have to fight to survive, you might as well appreciate your work. But consider how every age is defined by its art, and while the ancient Greeks had Homer, and the Renaissance had Michelangelo, the world you've inherited has for its iconic artist the guy who's filled his lawn sprinkler with hydrochloric acid. Is this really where you want to live?

Improvisation Medal
Unlocked!

AMMO   26

L Is for Leave Him Behind! He's Been Bitten!

Survive long enough and you will meet a fellow like Jerry, who has lost his entire family and every friend he's ever had but has somehow moved past grief to become the living embodiment of hope. Jerry has faced that long dark night of the soul and emerged determined to bring meaning and humanity back into the world. When he falls in with your own motley crew, you quickly learn that he's a great guy. Jerry always volunteers for sentry duty in the middle of the night, always agrees to join the risky supply run into the most infested regions of town and emerges unscathed with a clever remark and a few artful smudges on his cheeks and forehead. As long as Jerry's around, you know that you're all going to make it, that somehow the whole world's going to make it.

And then your entire group will be out foraging on the wrong side of the wrong fence. You'll bludgeon your way free and see the van you left behind for a quick getaway. You'll pile in and whirl around looking for Jerry and see that he's right behind you, reaching for you so you can pull him to safety. And you'll see the mingled hope and fear in his eyes and you'll know that you have only a heartbeat to act and you'll hesitate just long enough to see the dead woman in the nun's habit take a nice meaty chunk out of his arm.

And so you tell the guy behind the wheel to peel out.

You'll miss Jerry. But he knew the rules.

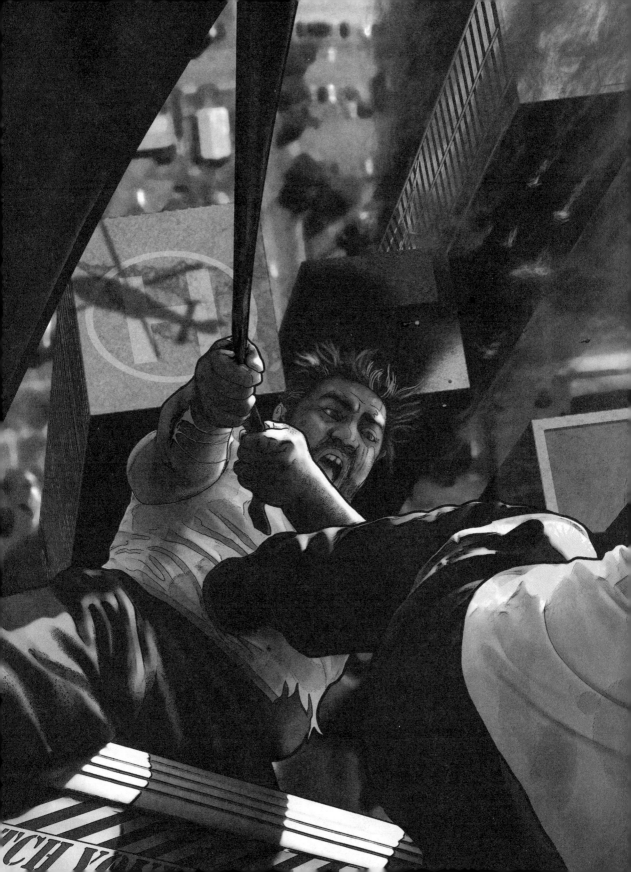

 Is for Mindless

The one major advantage you have is the void between the average zombie's ears. They know they're hungry, and they know that the screaming, running, baseball-bat-wielding things are their preferred food, but that's all they know. They don't know enough to stay out of the way of chain saws. They don't know enough to avoid the open manhole that bisects the straight line between them and you. They don't even know enough to get out of the way when you level your flaming explosive arrow. Knowledge is something they left behind when they died; learning is something they just don't do. The average goldfish, with its reputed two-second memory, has a steeper learning curve than the average zombie.

And yet the one sure way to put one down is to destroy its brain. The brain, which is no more intelligent in the average zombie than the cauliflower it resembles, generates just enough electrical activity to keep those legs moving, those hands grasping, and those jaws chewing. For some people you knew in the world before the rising of the dead, this qualifies as a major comedown. But for others, not so much. Some days, when you're roaming the streets in search of food, you watch the vacant-eyed, slack-jawed corpses jaywalking their way through eternity and you cannot avoid the hateful conclusion that for all too many of them, not that much has changed.

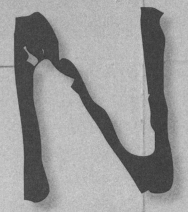

N Is for Need More Ammunition

In terms of mere physical skill, any one reasonably fit human being is more than a match for any one zombie. You need only a slight push to make one fall down, and as long as you stay away from the mouth yawning wide beneath uncomprehending eyes, you can kick them about with impunity, feeling like a martial arts champion even if you've never had so much as a single lesson. If you have a handgun, so much the better. For anybody with a modicum of aim, a single zombie is like the very first practice monster you encounter in a video game, before you move on to the next level and the opposition starts getting difficult.

But the terrible ecology of the world after the plague is stacked against you, because you'll never face just one zombie. You'll find yourself besieged on all sides, plinking away at the dead faces in front of you while being pawed by the dead hands behind you. You'll put a round through the eye of that snarling pink-pantsuited real estate saleswoman attempting to gnaw on your wrist with her blood-and-lipstick-stained teeth, and not have enough left in the clip to dispatch the wall of ravenous dead flesh just a few spastic steps behind her. A good flamethrower will eliminate an entire row of them at once, which is a vast improvement over the revolver's pathetic one at a time, but even there your resources remain nonrenewable, and the dead will continue to advance over the twitching corpses of the ones first in line.

This is the one terrible realization you'll come to as you do the math.

They're no longer people.

They're cockroaches.

10¢
1 AMAZING COMICS
Adam Smasher!
Jr. Zombie Hunter
Part Four:
Need more ammunition!

# Is for Omigod Omigod Oh Jesus Get It Off Me Get It Off Get It . . . Aaaarrrgggh

In the event they do catch up with you and you have no final bullet with which to spare yourself the agony of being devoured, you will find yourself in the position of speaking your last words. This is the last major decision of your life, and though it might not seem to you like it matters all that much, remember that you can go down being the person who snarled, "I hope you choke on me, you bastards," or the one who cried out the titular phrase while bawling like a little girl.

Since there may be other survivors around who will bring the tale of your final moments to others and possibly teach it to the generations destined to come of age in a world where nobody ever buries Grandma without drilling a hole through her skull first, it behooves you to spend a little time compiling a list of last defiant quips designed to leave people eulogizing you as a tragic hero and not as hapless cannon fodder who never stood a shot at being anything but some undead birthday clown's choice of luncheon meat. Among those that work, more or less, are "Drop dead *again*!" and "Yeah, why *don't* you eat me!" Among those you want to avoid, for posterity's sake, would be "Take the child first— she's more tender!"

P Is for Putrid

And then there's the smell.

Within hours of death, the body cavities evacuate. Decomposition begins. Tissues swell with noxious gases. Swollen bellies split open and release the acrid stench. Some of the substances spilled during a fight with a sufficiently aged zombie will affect your own personal aroma for days. Sure, you'll get desensitized after a while and be able to wade into a mob of the rotters without blinking, but it'll never be fun.

Now multiply that stomach-churning miasma by thousands, or millions.

Even if you're nestled in the mountains or high above the city streets, you better hope that you have top-of-the-line air filters . . . because the inescapable stench carries for miles. Or to put it another way, that hypothetical plucky group of survivors exchanging quips on the roof of the shopping mall, while thousands of dead people swarm below them? In real life they'd be down in the public restrooms, waiting for their stomach convulsions to fade. Because in the world after there's no more room in hell, the one god we'll all still kneel to is sparkly white and made out of porcelain.

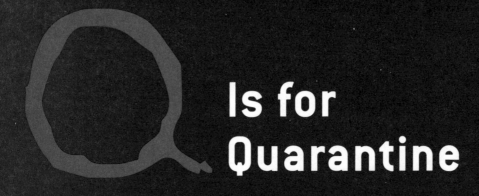

Is for
Quarantine

It has been a long and nightmarish six days. You have somehow fought your way free of the charnel house the city has become and joined the pitiful stream of refugees making its way to the base where the living have gathered to make their last stand. You see the gun towers and the barbed wire fence up ahead. You look at your fellow survivors in rags and think that the worst is over.

Get real.

If the people on the other side of the wall don't shoot you through the head just on general principle, they'll haul you off at rifle-point to sit within a fenced enclosure with thousands of others, while sentries on the walls watch through binoculars to see if you'll turn. Some of the people with you will. Every once in a while you'll hear a little commotion a few rows away as some guy wakes up from a temporary case of death and starts trying to take bites out of the refugees sitting next to him. The snipers will put a bullet through his head, ending the immediate threat, and the ghastly vigil will resume.

Don't think you're safe just because you're feeling fine. The snipers have been instructed to err on the side of caution. You might get misidentified as a fresh zombie just because you wake from a nap looking a little pale and wearing a stupid look on your face. Or you might just strike one of the bored snipers as a—please excuse the expression—dead ringer and acceptable substitute for the obnoxious brother-in-law who ruined every family holiday.

Keep saying to yourself that you only need to last for three days before you're awarded a clean bill of health. And try to look cheerful and lively, even though that lady next to you is looking a little green.

# Is for Ravenous

Here's the thing about zombies. They always eat. They never stop eating. They will eat even if they just ate. They will eat even if they don't have a body beneath the neck to feed. They will eat even if their abdomen's a gaping maw open to the elements and everything they ingest tumbles out looking only a little chewed. They will eat even if their bellies are bloated and distended with contents under pressure and one more bite of school bus driver might lead to an explosion of the sort that results in every nearby surface being plastered with abstract art. They will not be sufficiently satisfied with eating your friends to save you for later. Zombies don't fill up on bread. They don't stuff themselves on the appetizers and then stare at the expensive entrée, looking glum. They might not have room for more, but they're always willing to give it a game try. For them, it's always lunch hour, and they're always in line behind the guy who takes forever to order.

You're entitled to hate them for this, and not only because the ones who just dismembered and devoured your best friend are not about to say, "Enough already," and wander off, leaving you in some semblance of peace.

No. What really rankles is that so few of them are fat.

 Is for Shambling

Once upon a time, there was a series of popular movies about a monster known as Kharis the Mummy, who was always able to catch up with his fleeing victims even though he dragged one foot and seemed to pause for deep consideration before taking any step with the other. The average zombie can only wish for that kind of speed. The most intact move like drunks whose pants have been filled with Jell-O. This is in part due to the garbled nature of nerve impulses traveling through a body that's already started to rot, but also because many of them are not intact at all. They're coming for us even if they have shattered kneecaps, fractured tibias, broken necks, dislocated hips, and snapped tendons. They're coming for us even if they're little more than a brain and spine connected to a pair of legs. They're coming for us even if they can't lift their feet when taking a step and the only way to get to us is by climbing that flight of stairs. They're coming for us even if they've been flattened below the waist and need to drag themselves forward with arms that have already been worn down to the bones.

They didn't ask to be this way, and sometimes, when you look at zombies like the once-pretty girl in the bloody leotard who stumbles forward blindly on one intact leg and one that ends in splintered bone at the ankle, you almost find yourself feeling sorry for them. But the one thing you need to keep in mind is not that they're coming with the speed you would expect from creatures who have been rendered strangers in their own bodies. It's that they're coming. And that they won't stop.

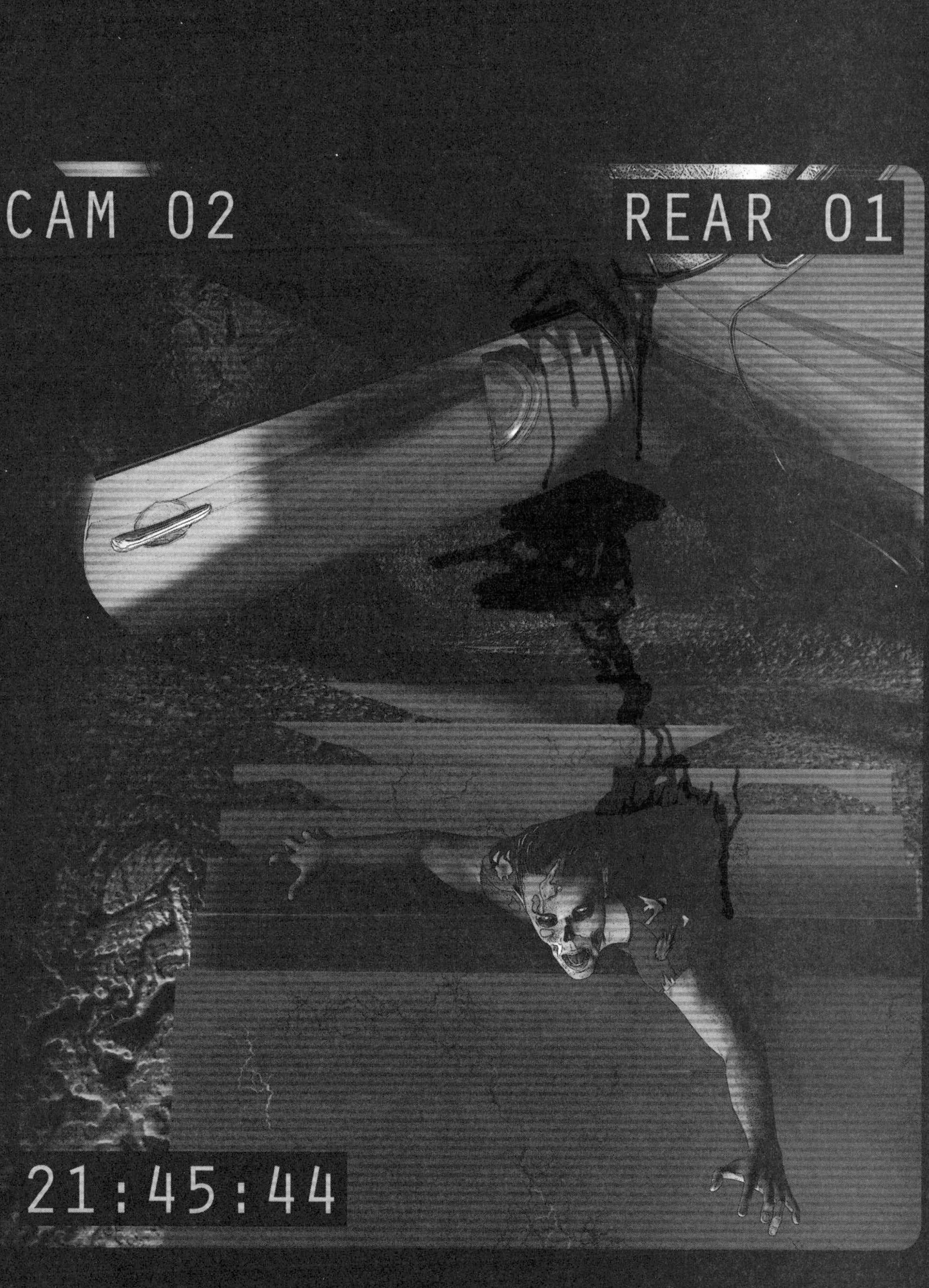
CAM 02
REAR 01
21:45:44

T Is for Terrifying

Not all zombies have eyes.

And if you're very, very lucky, most of your encounters with them will be from a safe distance, separated from their groping hands and gnashing teeth by a barrier of concrete walls.

But sooner or later you will see one close up, maybe even—if your luck's held out—through a pane of shatterproof glass.

And you will make eye contact. And you will have time to dwell on the sight, and you will discover that this may just be the worst aspect of life after the living dead.

People say that eyes are the windows to the soul. They say of their lovers that when they gaze into each other's eyes, they get lost in the beauty to be found there.

This can be seen as empty romanticism, the kind of observation you only get from poets and teenagers, and especially poets who also happen to be teenagers.

But a zombie's eyes are windows to nothing. The only thing behind those staring gray orbs is emptiness: a total vacuum unpolluted by awareness, empathy, intelligence, mercy, or spirit. It's a void so deep and so cold that for some the mere glimpse is enough to shatter all will to live, and not just because it lurks behind the very same eyes that in life belonged to your husband, or wife, or parent, or child.

It's just as terrifying when seen through the eyes of an undead stranger.

That's because what waits behind those eyes is your future.

Even if you live long enough to die of old age . . .

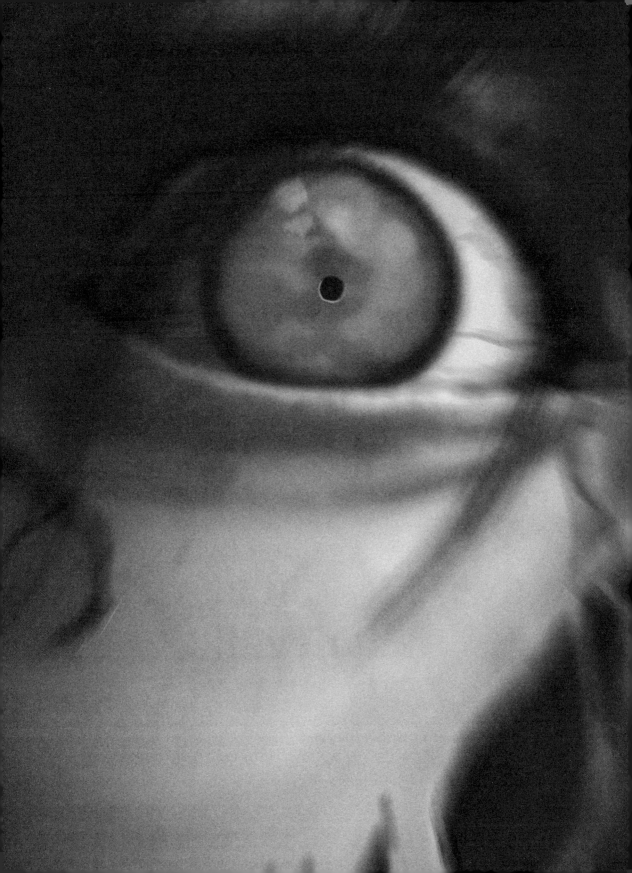

U Is for Unbearable

The moment will come.

If you've survived the collapse of your society and all its institutions; if you've fought your way clear of a civilization reduced to a slaughterhouse; if you've outlived your friends and family and everybody you ever loved; if you've become so inured to horror that you can walk knee-deep in blood without feeling something inside of you die; if you've become a killing machine capable of channeling your harshest instincts to commit acts that once would have left you sickened; if you've managed to repress your sense of repugnance at the sights and the smells and the sounds of a world that has plunged all the way to hell; if you've built up so many levels of emotional armor that you no longer feel horror at what necessity forces you to do just to get through every second of every minute of every day; if you've, at long last, lived long enough that the march of the living dead is no longer an obscenity to you, but just an everyday fact of life; if you're at home in it; then there will come a moment, maybe a quiet moment and maybe a moment in the midst of a raging battle, where the thought will slap you across the face like a scolding from an offended maiden aunt.

"Why?"

It's really not all that enviable a position, you know.

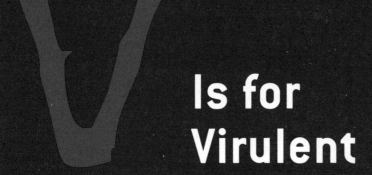

Is for Virulent

So let's say the zombies don't catch you. Let's say that you kick and behead and chain-saw and blow up and lawn-mower every single dead thing that makes the attempt, or even that you develop some kind of handy-dandy zombie repellent that makes you unappetizing to them.

Do you really think that means your life is going to be healthy?

Please. When civilization goes, the medical establishment goes. When the medical establishment goes, our defenses against epidemics go. And one thing any epidemic does is weaken the remaining population, leaving it vulnerable to other opportunistic pathogens.

Zombies are unburied corpses. Zombies are *rotting* unburied corpses. They're amusement parks for deadly bacteria, fast-food places for flies. You may never catch whatever it is that makes them get up and walk, but that still leaves you wide open to any number of other, possibly even more unpleasant things that they incubate and spread just by existing. It's very possible to fight off a swarm of dead postal workers with nothing but an axe and a few slick moves, prove how cool you are with a sardonic wisecrack, and then strut away thinking you've won but already be dying from the kind of bug you once tried to avoid by not drinking the water in certain countries.

Zombies are not just carnivorous ghouls from beyond the grave. They're medical waste.

So when you behead one, be sure to wash your hands.

W Is for War

It may happen in lots of different places, all over the world. And it may happen in only one: a Little Big Horn, a Waterloo, a Times Square. But if the war goes badly for us, there shall come a day when the last survivors prepare to make their last stand against the overwhelming forces of the living dead. They will look out upon a battlefield they haven't chosen, a war they never wanted, an enemy they don't understand. They will know that the chances are against them. They will know that they will almost certainly go down screaming, only to rise transformed in a world where there are no longer any living folks to eat.

They will level weapons that may include flamethrowers and rocket launchers and may be nothing more than rocks and sharp sticks, and they will position their backs against the nearest wall and listen with grim expectation as the chorus of unearthly moans grows louder.

Somebody will attempt to make a stirring speech, reminding them what they're fighting for and why they should give the next few minutes everything they have.

It might be a good speech. It might be a bad one. But it's really not very necessary. Anybody in the ranks who hasn't figured out what's at stake probably shouldn't have made it this far.

Either way, one thing's for sure. Nobody's given any zippy pep talks to the other side.

They always had all the motivation they needed.

Marks the Spot Where They Finally Catch Up with You

It's not going to be anyplace you want to be.

Zombies don't catch up with you when you're sipping margaritas at a tropical resort on a bright, sunny day. They don't catch up with you when you've just bowled the 7-10 split that wins the tournament for your league. They don't catch up with you when you've just won the Academy Award or Nobel Peace Prize, or after

you've finally gotten a yes from the one person you've loved from afar. For all you know, there might have been some people who got caught at such moments of transformative joy and never knew what hit them—people who died happy, back when it was possible to be happy, because the news about the rising of the dead hadn't reached them yet and winning five dollars on a scratch-off lottery ticket was still the kind of good luck capable of making one's day.

But if you've survived past the first attacks, past the mounting odds, and past the awful realization that the forces of the warm are losing, you won't be so blessed.

You'll go at the bottom of a garbage-strewn flight of stairs, with your right leg twisted at a strange angle and a tidal wave of dead people descending toward you.

You'll go starving in a bunker after the food runs out, with no way of ending your misery except opening the door to the dozens who've spent the last few weeks pacing back and forth on the other side.

You'll go shivering against a chain-link fence in winter, while the slack-jawed faces of people who used to be your friends draw ever closer for a group hug that won't leave you feeling any warmer.

Trust us on this.

By the time the inevitable happens, it will almost be a blessing.

Is for Your Transformation

And now you've been bitten. You've managed to avoid being torn to pieces and have crawled off to some isolated place where you can face the rest of your living existence in privacy. You've already been through your stages of denial, bargaining, and anger. Now you're well into acceptance. The site of the wound rages with infection. Your throat's gone dry and your head's spinning with fever.

In your delirium you see the faces of your loved ones loom before you, not as you saw them last, blue and bloated and stained with the juice of the people they ate before you found them, but alive and well and laughing the way they did at life's best moments. You weep and you apologize to them for not being able to do better. They tell you it's okay, really, it won't be all that bad. Everything that made you sad in the old world will be going away soon. Everything that troubled you will join it. You'll no longer feel any confusion over what's right and what's wrong or whether you said the right thing or even whether there happen to be any unsightly substances between your teeth.

In a way, you reflect, you're almost lucky. You lived for as long as there was any point in living and then let go when that shred of solace was all that remained. You dread the next part but realize now that there's little point in that.

What will rise, in a little while, may be an obscene parody of you, but you won't be around to take offense.

You can't feel your legs.
Your breath catches. Your
heart thumps. The world
turns dark at the edges and
then contracts, like an iris
closing on the final image in
a silent movie. A smile curls
the corners of your lips. Here
it comes. In just a couple of
moments, you'll be at peace.
Your heart stops.
Darkness embraces you.
And the next thing you know,
you discover exactly how wrong you were.

Z Is for Zombie

It turns out that being one is even worse than you ever imagined.

You remember everything. You understand everything.

You know what you are.

You even know what you're eating, and who you're eating.

But this is all you have to look forward to.

Welcome to the new world.

Acknowledgments

Adam-Troy Castro

With many of my previous books I questioned whether there was anybody in the world who really reads the acknowledgments and learned that the answer is "Yes, of course, those likely to be upset they aren't mentioned." Among those who are not given reason to be upset here are my wife, Judi; my agents Eddie Schneider and Joshua Bilmes of the Jabberwocky Literary Agency; my editor, Diana Gill; Will Hinton; and my collaborator, Johnny Atomic of League Entertainment, whose images will pop your eyes out of your head. I also thank the various members of the South Florida Science Fiction Society Writer's Workshop, a group that includes Brad Aiken, Dave Dunn, Chris Negelein, and David Slavin. Thanks also to John Scalzi, Jonathan Maberry, Mira Grant, and John Skipp, who previewed the manuscript. And finally, thanks to George Romero, who first disturbed the freshly packed earth. If I left any names out it is no doubt due to the slower thought processes that go along with my imminent transformation.

Johnny Atomic

Ken Chapman	League Entertainment
Maria Chapman	League Entertainment
Jason Torres	League Entertainment
Rob Westerfield	Westerfield Studios
Diana Gill	For taking a chance
Jabberwocky	For getting it out there
Larry Aramanda	For providing "The Button"
Mike Hill	For everything
John Perry	For everything else
And Dave Zeien	(For reasons known only to himself)

Special Credit

Kris Renta

Courtney Nawara

Gabriel Jackson

Chance Jackson

Julian Jackson

Shelley Jackson

Victor Hoskin

"Blue"

And the mighty Christian Palamaro

Love

Adam and Judi Castro

Z IS FOR

ZOMBIE

Adam-Troy Castro (writer) is an internationally acclaimed author of fantasy, science fiction, and horror. He has been nominated for two Hugos, five Nebulas, and two Bram Stoker Awards, his most recent award nomination being the Stoker nod for his terrifying novella *The Shallow End of the Pool.* His previous seventeen books include the science fiction thrillers *Emissaries from the Dead* and *The Third Claw of God. Emissaries* won the Philip K. Dick Award. Adam lives in Miami with his wife, Judi, and a motley assortment of cats that includes Meow Farrow and Uma Furman. Readers interested in finding out more about his projects can check out his website at www.sff.net/people/adam-troy.

Johnny Atomic (artist) is the cofounder of the wildly successful concept house League Entertainment. He is the cocreator of the popular Choose Your Doom interactive story series as well as the Simon Vector comic book series.